AuthorHouse™
1663 Liberty Drive
Bloomington, IN 47403
www.authorhouse.com
Phone: 833-262-8899

Because of the dynamic nature of the Internet, any web addresses or links contained in this book may have changed since publication and may no longer be valid. The views expressed in this work are solely those of the author and do not necessarily reflect the views of the publisher, and the publisher hereby disclaims any responsibility for them.

Any people depicted in stock imagery provided by Getty Images are models, and such images are being used for illustrative purposes only.
Certain stock imagery © Getty Images.

This book is printed on acid-free paper.

ISBN: 978-1-5246-5506-8 (sc)
978-1-5246-5507-5 (e)

Library of Congress Control Number: 2020911341

Print information available on the last page.

Published by AuthorHouse 01/28/2021

authorHOUSE

The Heart Is Not a GarBage Can

Miriam Ahuva Schecter, LCSW

David had a BIG problem.

Bigger than he even realized.

David lived in a three-family house.

He lived on the first floor, the Miller family lived on the second floor, and Mr. Gold lived on the third floor.

All three neighbors shared a main lobby.

Every day when David would come home after a long day of school, he was greeted by a rather foul odor.

It smelled like garbage had been sitting around for a very long time.

The smell was so bad that he would have to hold his nose until his mother opened the door to their apartment and let him in.

You must be wondering where this rotten odor came from. In order to answer that question, I will have to tell you more about Mr. Gold. He was a widower and a retired chef. However, he still loved to cook and bake, and so he spent his days puttering in his kitchen, concocting the most delectable recipes.

When Mr. Gold was finished cooking or baking, he was left with loads of garbage. Unfortunately, climbing down three flights of stairs to take out his garbage was a very difficult venture. Therefore, he would postpone taking out his garbage each day.

Instead, he would fill his garbage can until there was not an inch of space left. Then he would shove the garbage down with a broom to make more room and stuff it with even more garbage!

Finally, at the end of the week, Mr. Gold was left with no choice: **he had to take his garbage out!**

The same scenario would repeat itself week after week, which went as follows:

Mr. Gold would start his trek down the three flights of stairs, carrying a bulging and smelly garbage bag.

By the time he was down the first flight, Mr. Gold would hear a ripping sound. He looked down and saw a little hole forming at the edge of the bag. "Oh, no!" he cried, as the egg yolks slowly dribbled down the stairs.

Mr. Gold hurried down the second flight of stairs.

By now the little hole had grown larger, and potato peels and chicken bones were slipping out.

Mr. Gold dashed as fast as he could (which was never fast enough) into the main lobby, and just as he had his hand on the front door, he would hear a loud

"BOOM!"

"OH, NO!" wailed Mr. Gold.

To his dismay, the garbage bag had exploded all over the floor! Mr. Gold was now left with the daunting task of cleaning up this huge mess.

"How silly of me," moaned Mr. Gold.

"If only I had not waited soooooooo long to take out my garbage. If only I had not been soooooooo lazy, I would not have all this hard work."

It must have taken Mr. Gold an hour to clean up.
Of course, it was hard for him to bend down, and so some of the garbage remained on the floor.

And that, my dear readers, is how the awful smell appeared week after week.

One day, David came home from school with a friend, who was overwhelmed by the smell and gave David a pitying glance. David was embarrassed that his house smelled. He decided that he was going to solve this odor problem once and for all!

He thought long and hard and came up with a brilliant plan. Quickly, he ran up the three flights of stairs and knocked urgently on Mr. Gold's door.

"Who's there?" called Mr. Gold.

"It's David, your downstairs neighbor," responded the boy.

Mr. Gold opened the door.

"What can I do for you?" asked Mr. Gold.

"Are you selling cookies like your sister?"

"No, no, I came to..." David paused.

He wasn't sure how to present his idea in a respectful way.

He cleared his throat, "Um..., um, I noticed that it's hard for you to walk down the stairs..., and I was thinking that I could come by after school and give you a hand and take your garbage out for you."

Mr. Gold blushed a little and smiled. "Yes," he said, "it is difficult for me.... Well, I don't want to trouble you. You are very kind to make such an offer, but I—"

David interrupted, "Please, Mr. Gold, it's no big deal. I will come by tomorrow after school."

He then dashed back down the stairs to his apartment.

David was true to his word, so the very next day he took Mr. Gold's garbage out.

The garbage bag was very light, since it had only a day's worth of garbage.

He continued this every day.

So, dear readers, what do you think happened?

Do you think David solved his problem?

Do you think the odor went away?

It sure seems so.

Mr. Gold was quite pleased, as well as the Millers on the second floor, for there were no more garbage bags exploding all over the main lobby.

The smell eventually disappeared, and everyone was able to breathe more easily.

Our story should end here..., **but it doesn't!**

"Why not?" you ask.

The truth is that our story is just unfolding.

Little did David realize that he was just beginning to solve

his problem.

Taking out Mr. Gold's garbage was the easy part.

What happens next in our story is where

David will need to work really hard.

A few weeks later, David had one of those weeks that went from bad to worse.

(Ever have one of those weeks?)

It started on a Monday, with a yucky lunch.

David came down to the lunchroom and opened up his lunchbox.To his dismay, he found tuna patties and stringbeans inside.

"Ugh! What a terrible lunch!" he muttered under his breath.

As his stomach growled from hunger, he watched everyone else eat their yummy lunches.

David was feeling _____ .

(Fill in the blank.)

When he came home from school, he put his lunchbox on the kitchen counter with a huff!

But he didn't say anything to his Mom.

On Tuesday, he was playing soccer in the gym, when he missed a really easy goal.

His team lost by one point.

One kid on his team shoved him in the ribs and yelled, "You stink at soccer!"

David was feeling _____ .
(Fill in the blank.)

His teammate had no right to bully him like that.

Yet, David said nothing and skulked back to his classroom.

On Wednesday, David's math teacher returned an exam. David hated math. He had missed playing basketball with the kids on his block and instead spent days studying. When the teacher called out David's name, he nervously took the test and looked at his mark. To his chagrin, there was a big red circle on top of his test with a 65 on it! David could not believe his eyes!

He knew he was not a math whiz, but he expected at least to pass. After quickly scanning his test, he noticed that he had left out the entire second page. David remembered asking his math teacher why the test skipped from question 16 to 32, but his teacher just ignored him. He realized now that the pages were stuck together, so he had only done pages 1 and 3.

David was feeling _____. (fill in the blank).
However, he just stuffed his test into his backpack and said nothing to his teacher.

On Thursday, he came home to an empty house.

Posted on the fridge was a note that said that his Mom had to attend an emergency meeting, so he should baby-sit his little sister.

His sister was a big pest and whined for hours and hours! He felt like his head was about to roll off from all the noise.

He was feeling _____.
(Fill in the blank.)

When his Mom finally came home, he quickly ran to his room and went to bed.

Yet, he didn't say anything to his Mom.

On Friday, his science teacher handed out a sheet with a complex assignment for the Science Fair. It was on a topic he hated, Sedimentary Rocks.

"How boooooooooring! There goes my peaceful weekend!" he thought, as he left his classroom and headed toward the school bus.

He was feeling _____.

(Fill in the blank.)

Yet, he said nothing to his teacher and just stuffed all his feelings deep inside his heart.

As David stepped off the bus, there was a large gray cloud hanging over him. When he walked through the door of his apartment, he dropped his backpack on the floor. His mother greeted him with a smile, and said, "David, I am so glad you are home. I could really use your help unpacking the groceries."

David's face turned red as he flew into a rage.

"Don't tell me what to do!" he roared.

"I am not unpacking any groceries. Not today, not ever!!" he bellowed.

With a huff and a puff, he stormed up to his room and slammed his door shut.

His mother stood frozen in disbelief.

What happened?

She always asks David to help unpack the groceries, and he always does it happily.

What did she say wrong?

David was in his room, pacing back and forth.

His heart was pounding, and his mind was racing.

David's little sister knocked on his door.

"David, can I borrow your—"

"Go away!" barked David. "Leave me alone!"

David's sister ran to her mother, crying.

Meanwhile, David's anger continued to brew, and in a rage he started to knock down the things that were lying on his dresser. His collection of baseball cards was scattered all over the floor.

His anger escalated over the next hour, and his room looked as if a tornado had hit it!

Suddenly, there was a loud thud.

David jumped.

"What was that noise?"

He ran downstairs to check it out for himself.

The front door was open, and his mother and sister were standing with surprised looks on their faces.

David looked into the lobby, and there was poor Mr. Gold, holding a busted garbage bag with its contents splattered all over the floor!

David was staring at the smelly garbage strewn all over the floor, when a sharp thought, like a bolt of lightning, ran through his head, and then everything made sense to him. Within seconds, David began to cry.

Mr. Gold ran over to David and put his arm around him. "Please, don't cry," Mr. Gold said. "It's not your responsibility to take out my garbage. You must have had a busy week."

David looked up at Mr. Gold and replied, "No! No! I am not crying because I forgot to take out **your garbage.** I am crying because I forgot to take out **my garbage!**"

Here is a good place to pause and start an interactive discussion. The following are some excellent questions to get the children thinking:

1. What garbage is David referring to as his own?

2. What would be an analogy for a garbage can in a human being?

3. Have you ever exploded like David?

4. What happens when we leave garbage inside us for too long?

5. Why is it so hard to take out the garbage from our hearts?

6. Describe David's explosion. Do you think there are other ways people explode? What are they?

The following question can be saved for a later discussion. This question is for a more mature group, such as teens.

7. Are explosions always external, or can they happen internally? Give some examples of internal explosions.

This is an excellent time to explain the concept of "mind-body connection" and how stuffed emotions can turn inside the body and present themselves as symptoms such as headaches, stomachaches, back tension, chronic fatigue, etc.

"What are you talking about?" asked Mr. Gold. "I don't understand."

"The whole week," David replied, "I've been having frustrating events take place, and each time I just stuffed all my feelings back into my heart."

Then he added, "I exploded, and leaked my stinky garbage all over my poor mother and sister!"

He then turned to his Mom and little sis and apologized for yelling at them.

Mr. Gold looked on with pride and gently said, "David, I have a proposal to make that will solve your problem. You have been so kind to me and have been helping me take out my garbage each day, so I will help you take out your garbage each day."

David looked quizzically at Mr. Gold.

"Now I don't understand you," said David.

Mr. Gold explained, "I will prepare my famous chocolate chip cookies, and you can eat them as you share the events of your day. Sharing your feelings can make you hungry!

After you share with me what is bothering you, you will be emptying your heart of all the negativity, and you will feel much lighter and happier!"

David loved the idea.

He went each day after school to speak with Mr. Gold, who was an excellent listener. He never interrupted, he just nodded his head with empathy. He didn't even give David advice on how to deal with his frustrations.

Somehow, just by talking things out, David felt the heaviness lifting off his chest.

Once he shared the ups and the downs of his day, he was in a much better frame of mind to come up with some helpful solutions to his problems.

David and Mr. Gold became good friends as they helped each other take out their garbage and lighten each other's load!

THE END!

This is another good time to get the children into a lively discussion. The following are some excellent questions:

1. What was Mr. Gold's suggestion for David to help him take out the garbage from his heart? Do you think that was a good idea?

2. Would that help you? Why or why not?

3. Do you have other ideas for David that would help him take out his garbage?

4. What would you advise David to do in the future to prevent him from having a repeat of his explosion?

5. What are some things you do to help yourself take out the garbage from your heart?

6. Do you think David's problem was solved? Do you think he will never explode at his family again? Why or why not?

7. What are some obstacles you find in sharing your problems with others?

8. Do you have a certain individual in your life who you find it's easier to talk to? What is it about that person that makes you want to share your troubles with her or him?

9. Do you think the analogy of garbage in the heart pertains only to negative feelings like anger or jealousy, or can it also pertain to positive feelings like excitement and pride?

If so, explain.

Activity:

Return to the part of the story that takes place from Monday to Friday, and ask the children to write their own twist of the story. Have them write a scenario for each day. After they write about a difficult week (they will usually use their personal life experiences), have them read what they wrote out loud. This is a great way to start having the children share their problems in a nonthreatening way. Some of my clients have requested that I print out a copy of their version of the book and substitute their name for David's.

I offer a gold coin for each event shared and announce to the child that he or she is:

"Transforming their garbage into gold!"

The Benefits of using this story in therapy with clients:

After twenty years of using this story successfully with children of all ages, I felt compelled to share it with the public. This book can be read to children, teens, and adults, for the analogy of using one's heart as a garbage can is pertinent for all ages.

I found that many of my clients were confused about what "therapy" is all about. They did not understand the point of talking about their problems. Many clients would ask, "How is talking about my problems going to help me?" Or they might say, "I spoke about this before, so why do I have to talk about it again?" I have found that this story offers a concrete analogy of what happens when we stuff our feelings and never talk about them with another person.

Sadly, so many people go through life with heavy hearts, keeping all their problems inside them, thinking they won't affect them in the future. What I have witnessed with so many of my clients is that those feelings do not go away. Instead, they just end up collecting inside their hearts for years and years, manifesting themselves in emotional illnesses that disrupt the clients' relationships and emotional health. The clients then end up suffering from anxiety and depression and many psychosomatic illnesses. They thought there was some deep mystery to their symptoms, when they had simply abused their hearts and turned them into smelly garbage cans. Unfortunately, by the time the clients got to me, their hearts were like garbage dumps that required years of therapy to clean out.

It is my hope that this book will motivate people to consistently take out the garbage in their hearts with a close friend or a professional and not wait until they explode, hurting themselves and those they love!

About the Author:

Hi! My name is Miriam Ahuva Schecter, and I live in Baltimore, Maryland, with my five sons. The message I try to impart to myself, my family, and clients is: "We need to thrive, not just survive!" I strongly believe that the key to thriving is *Friendship.* Throughout my life, no matter how challenging, I have been blessed with friendships that have nurtured and restored me.

I began the first four years of my career as a Child Educator and observed firsthand children interacting with their peers. It pained me to watch how many children struggled socially and how this negatively impacted their emotional health. After earning my LCSW, I opened my private practice and began to facilitate social skills groups for children. I called my first group the "Friendship Hour." Over the next two decades, I developed a comprehensive program that helped many children develop both socially and emotionally. Parents, teachers, and principals all shared their appreciation for this much needed program.

I also realized early on that, for many clients, especially those who have been through abuse and trauma, they did not have the words to unload the "garbage from their hearts." Some of my clients, such as adult survivors of childhood abuse, didn't even have the conscious memories of the "garbage" they had endured. I sought out a form of therapy that would help my clients "purge" without words. I was very fortunate to attend Stephanie Haggadorn's Sandtray Certificate program. Sandtray provided all my clients, regardless of age, culture, or gender, a powerful avenue to share their feelings in ways that traditional "talk therapy" could not offer.

In addition to the Sandtray therapy, I have always tried to incorporate another passion of mine, Art, into my therapy "tool box." From a very young age, I began discovering the many benefits of Art as a form of healing. I invested in years of training in Art techniques such as Oil, Acrylic, Watercolor, Silk Dyes, Stained Glass, Mosaics, and even Makeup Art. Each one has been a source of tremendous self-growth and self-expression, and I wanted to share it with my clients, even those who insisted they were not artistic. I incorporated my previous trainings and developed several "Intuitive Art Techniques" that I have been using successfully with many of my clients.

After many years, I returned to my original passion for teaching and became a Licensed Clinical Supervisor and Continuing Education Provider. What I discovered is that every person heals in his or her own unique way, and that there are many "keys" to the heart. My goal is to offer mental health professionals some of the powerful "keys" that I have been using with my clients over the last twenty years. I offer three CE comprehensive trainings in: Sandtray Therapy, Intuitive Art Techniques, and Social Skills Therapy.

I have been very blessed to teach many wonderful therapists over the years, heralding from Texas, New York, New Jersey, Virginia, Maryland, etc. I am very proud of their commitment to invest in their clinical skills as they tenaciously strive to enhance the healing journey for their clients! If you, too, would like to explore some new modalities, please visit my website:

www.thrivecenterbaltimore.org

I would like to thank all my dear friends, therapists, and mentors who have guided me throughout the "good and bad times" in my life.

A special thanks to my Mom, Stephanie Haggadorn, and Sara Leah Frid for encouraging me to develop my talents and share them with others.

Thank you, Eli, Meir, Ahron, Baruch, and Hershel for being my "lighthouses." You pump life into my heart each and every day!

Thank you to all my brave clients and students, who infuse me with inspiration.

Thank you, G-d, for sending me loads of helpers to continuously expand, educate, nurture, and strengthen my heart as I travel through the exciting adventures of love and friendship. Your many gifts are a constant reminder to me that you are holding my heart in your hands and watching over me every step of the way!

Sincerely,

Miriam Ahuva

Printed in the United States
By Bookmasters